This book belongs to

_____

Characters
Narrator            Jim Wise
Dax Lo              Louis Carazo
Andrew Hartford     Adrian Alita
Ronny Robinson      Karen Jean Olds
Will Aston          Sean Spann
Rose Ortiz          Laura Simms
Max Hartford        Rufus Gates
Moltor              RT Vader
Flurious            Tom Bo

Song:
Power Rangers Operation Overdrive
Main Theme (01:00)
Written by Terrance Yoshiaki, Mike Fratantuno,
Brian Lapin and Josef Lord
© 2007 Walt Disney Music Company (ASCAP)/
Wonderland Music Company Inc. (BMI)
All Rights Reserved. Used by Permission.
℗ 2007 Buena Vista Records

Read-Along Produced by Randy Thornton
and Ted Kryczko
Engineered by Dan Montes and Jeff Sheridan
Read-Along adaptation by Greg Ehrbar

℗ 2007 Buena Vista Records

This is a Parragon book
First published in 2007
Parragon
Queen Street House
4 Queen Street
Bath, BA1 1HE, UK

ISBN 978-1-4075-0443-8
Manufactured in China
TM and © 2007 BVS Entertainment, Inc.

Bath · New York · Singapore · Hong Kong · Cologne · Delhi · Melbourne

Beneath a sunny Hollywood sky, movie stuntman Dax Lo dispatched a trio of pursuers with the best moves in the business. His ability to climb walls and leap railings seemed to defy gravity.

Yet since he doubled for the star, Dax never got a camera close-up, or the leading lady's attention.

"I could've kissed her. I know how to kiss. He doesn't even know how to run!"

Dax lost his train of thought as he noticed a DVD device on his tiny cast chair. The holographic image of a man looked up at him. "I'm quite a fan of yours, Dax. I'm Andrew Hartford ... "

At the Grand Championship stock car race in Italy, world-class racer Ronny Robinson crossed the finish line to yet another triumphant win.

But as she peered inside the winner's trophy, she found a small DVD device, playing a very strange message.

"Congratulations, Ronny. I knew you'd win. You always do ... I'm Andrew Hartford."

South of the border, Will Aston slipped upside down into a high security Brazilian bank with the agility of a panther. Using a hand-held decoder, he unlocked the safe only to find what seemed to be the wrong item.

"What's this? I thought I was recovering the stolen Corinthian diamonds for the museum!"

The DVD beamed its message. "Nice job, Will! I hired you to break into my own vault in order to test your skills … you passed, with flying colours."

Far across the globe, at a London university, students run for cover as an experimental robotic arm swings wildly out of control. The professor struggles to override the piloting mechanism and stop the hysterical havoc.

Calmly ducking the beams, student Rose Ortiz nudges the professor away. In a few keyboard clicks, the problem is solved. "Professor. Next time you want to mess with my robot ... please don't!"

A DVD player fell out of her backpack. "Hello, Rose. I've read your papers on advanced nuclear robotic science. Very impressive ..."

Days later, upon invitation to Andrew Hartford's cavernous mansion, the foursome were welcomed by the billionaire explorer. They gasped as, on a huge monitor, he showed them video images that seemed too horrendous to be true: a fiery meteor descended to earth and a hideous being rose from the blaze. It was Moltor. He and his Lava Lizards were terrorizing innocent citizens.

Next, they saw a swirling snowstorm, from which Moltor's brother, Flurious, led his Chillers to cause widespread panic.

All of this horror had begun three days earlier, when Hartford unearthed the Corona Aurora – a legendary, five-jewelled crown with tremendous powers.

Hartford explained as the video continued to play. "Millennia ago, in a galaxy on the other side of the universe, there were two brothers ... "

Rose suddenly broke in. "Moltor and Flurious, who tried to steal the Corona Aurora. But the crown was so powerful; it cursed them and changed their appearance and sent them off to distant planets, imprisoning them in their own elements. I took a year of ancient universal legends at Harvard. Anyway, it's just a myth."

Hartford knew it was no myth. He explained that, had it not been for a wise and powerful being called the Guardian, all might have been lost. "In order to stop anyone from getting the power again, the Guardian took the five jewels from the crown and scattered them on a distant, uninhabited planet. That planet, those many millennia ago, was Earth."

"The four of you have the physical and mental qualities needed. And I have the technology and the money to fight this evil. I can turn you into Power Rangers."

Dax was pumped. "Power Rangers? YES!"

As he opened his safe and showed his team the Corona Aurora, Hartford was unaware that Moltor was watching on his own viewing screen deep in a fiery lair.

The villain growled. "Excellent! Gather round, my lizards. Now go and bring me back my crown!"

Moltor was also monitoring the actions of Flurious. He felt no obligation to his brother. He wanted the crown to be his and his alone.

In his secret tech lab, far below his mansion, Hartford used genetic re-sequencing to enhance the powers of his new team. "As your body adapts, you will soon be able to do things and know things that only moments ago were thought impossible."

Hartford was about to be re-sequenced himself when his son, Mack, burst into the lab. He had heard everything. "I knew something was going on!"

"I know, I know."

"You messed up big time. And I want to help. I want to be a Power Ranger, too."

But Hartford didn't want his son to get hurt. "No."

Outside, on the mansion grounds, Will was the first to notice his powers taking effect. "Did you guys hear that? It's so loud. And my eyesight – it's telescopular! Like right now, I see something moving in those bushes!"

In a flash, they all saw them. The Lava Lizards were attacking!

Ronny started to move. "I don't know about you guys, but I'm not goin' to sit here and be lizard food." To their amazement, Ronny zoomed at super speed! "Look out, Dax!"

Dodging a lizard, Dax sprung a hundred feet into the air!

Two lizards tried to charge at Rose, but instead bumped into each other. "Cool! I'm invisible!"

With the Lava Lizards temporarily out of the way, Hartford sent the team on the move, by all-terrain vehicle, jeep and motorbikes. But now, with the Chillers in pursuit, he handed each of the four an Overdrive Tracker. "These are what will morph you into Power Rangers."

After a false start, they matched up their moves and activated their Trackers. "OVERDRIVE, ACCELERATE!"

Bolts of energy coursed through their bodies as uniforms and helmets formed over them. In a flash of pink, yellow, blue and black, now Rose, Ronny, Dax and Will were Power Rangers.

But before Hartford could transform, the Chillers overcame him and he dropped his Tracker.

Mack snapped it up. "OVERDRIVE, ACCELERATE!"

Now the Red Ranger, Mack discovered he could choose a sword mode to nab a Chiller. "Drive lance!"

Black Ranger defended himself with a giant hammer. "Drive slammer!"

Blue Ranger used his powerful turbine fan to sprawl into the air and repel the Chillers and returning Lava Lizards. "Drive vortex!"

Yellow Ranger produced huge shovels that scooped up creatures and sent rocks flying. "Can you ice cubes dig this?"

Pink Ranger propelled her adversaries away with the powerful water jet device. "Drive geyser! Ya!"

Red Ranger spun his lance. "Red line time, heeeay!"

Lava Lizards flew in all directions.

But Moltor had already grabbed the Corona Aurora from Hartford's butler, Spencer. "Finally! The crown is mine!"

To make sure the Rangers wouldn't pursue him, Moltor created a volcano just above the city. "You want to be heroes? Be heroes!" Cascades of boiling lava oozed down toward the city's residents. Black Ranger swooped down to assist a young woman who had fallen in the mad rush to escape. Red Ranger tore open a car to rescue a mother and her baby just inches from the blaze.

At the volcano's source, Yellow used her shovels to blast through the crust, Blue's turbines kept things cool and Red's water jets pelted the lava into harmless rock.

Black, Red and the crowd were cornered by the lava, but Red had an idea. "Do you have your slammer handy?"

"Oh yeah! It's right here!" Black Ranger cut a gaping canyon in the street, allowing the lava to drain away completely. The crowd cheered the heroes.

Not only was Moltor defeated, he had also stolen a false crown. But as Hartford opened his office safe and held the real one, Moltor was right behind him. "Very clever. Now I'll take the real crown."

Mack found Hartford's office in ruins and his father gone. Rose tracked his location to the island of Rotuma. "Now, what I don't know is how we're going to get all the way over there."

Spencer showed the group to 'The Shark', a hydro aero recon craft, which skimmed them over the ocean in minutes.

But they weren't the only ones to land on the beach – and once again, it was time to tangle with the Lava Lizards before heading to rescue Hartford from the volcano cave.

As Moltor's prisoner Hartford was inside, held over the ledge of a cavernous lava pit. "I'll give you one more chance to come to your senses. Will you help me find the jewels or not?"

When Hartford refused, Moltor threw the explorer into the searing pit. Dax hit the scene just in time. "Zip line, go!"

Dax shot a grappling hook into the ceiling and swung over the pit in time to catch Hartford in mid fall. "That was the same stunt I did in *King for a Day*, only that time I saved a beautiful princess."

Mack was outside the cave battling Lava Lizards when Dax and Hartford found him. He reached for his Overdrive Tracker, much to Hartford's surprise. "Sorry Dad, you'll have to finish yelling at me later."

The five heroes assembled and synched their moves. "OVERDRIVE, ACCELERATE!"

As the Rangers switched from sword mode to weapon mode against the Lava Lizards, Red faced off with Moltor himself.

"Do you know who you're dealing with?"

"Do you? I'm just getting started!"

The defeated Moltor was enraged as he caught the exhaust of the departing Shark vehicle. "You'll pay for this! My creature will destroy this island and the people who live here!"

But as soon as they returned to the base, Hartford and the Rangers detected a giant sea creature back at the island. "Guys, get your Drive Megazords and go."

Mack watched anxiously as the four heroes grabbed their steering mechanisms. "Dad, they need my help."

Hartford looked at his new friends, who nodded in his support. Hartford nodded his approval. "Mack. Be careful."

Red Ranger climbed aboard a massive dump truck. "Dump Driver!"

Black Ranger revved up a powerful race car. "Speed Driver!"

Blue grabbed the controls of a hovercraft. "Yeah! Gyro Driver!" And with Yellow starting up the Dozer Driver, and Pink in the Sub Driver, they were ready for action.

"Drive Max Zords, move out!"

The sea creature spewed deadly lasers at the oncoming Zords. But Red used the Zord claws like giant pinchers, sending the creature to the ground. "That slowed him down. Let's stop him for good!"

All five Rangers activated the Drive Max Megazord, fusing all five super vehicles into one tremendous fighting machine.

The Megazord dug a huge pit, and then wielded a spectacular saber to drive off the creature. Moltor sent up an explosive shield on the beast. "We've got to get away from it!"

Using the legs of the Megazord to grab the creature, they flung it into the distance and into a burst of its own flames.

On another part of the island, the two brothers blamed each other. Flurious offered to take the crown, but Moltor refused. "It will be a cold day in my lava pit when that happens."

Angered, Flurious sent Moltor off in a shower of sparks. Each began attacking the other in a battle of lances and kicks more fierce than those between their foes. "It's every man for himself!"

His heroic deeds done, Mack turned in his Tracker.

Hartford handed it back. "I'm still not crazy about the idea, but I won't stop you. I hate to admit it, but you look better in red than I do." He authorized Mack for genetic re-sequencing.

With his new superhuman strength, Mack was able to lift Spencer with one hand – until Hartford said to put him down. "Listen up, Rangers. It's time to get to work. Our enemies have the crown and now they're going to be after the jewels. It's going to be the mission of Operation Overdrive to find them first!"

"Yeah!"

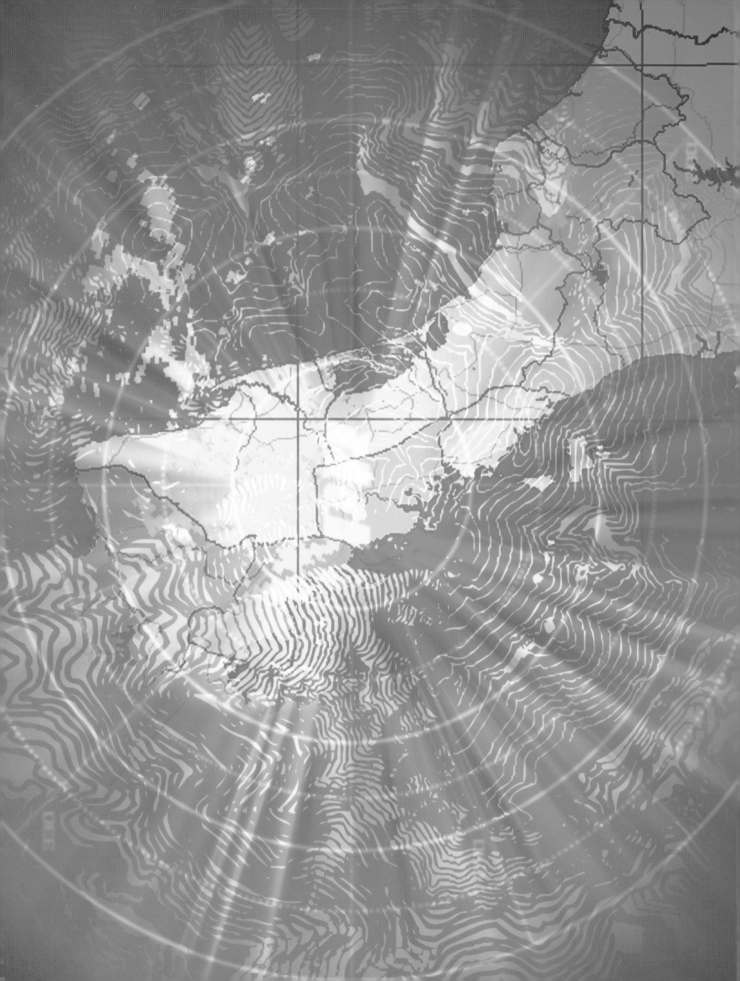